I CAN READ IT ALL BY MYSELF

Beginner Books

I Am NOT Going to Get up Today!

By Dr. Seuss
illustrated by James Stevenson

COLLINS

Trademark of Random House, Inc. William Collins Sons & Co Ltd, Authorised User.

1 2 3 4 5 6 7 8 9 10

ISBN 0 00 195787 – 2 (Paperback)
ISBN 0 00 195786 – 4 (Hardback)

Text copyright © 1987 Theodor S. Geisel and Audrey S. Geisel
Illustrations copyright © 1987 by James Stevenson.
Published by arrangement with
Random House Inc. New York, New York
First published in Great Britain in 1988.

Printed in Great Britain by
William Collins Sons and Co. Ltd Glasgow

I Am NOT Going to Get up Today!

Please let me be.

Please go away.

I am NOT going to get up today!

The alarm can ring.

The birds can peep.

My bed is warm.

My pillow's deep.

Today's the day I'm going to sleep.

I don't care if kids are getting up
right now all over town.
I'm the kid who ISN'T getting up.
I'm staying down.

All around the world
they're getting up.
And that's okay with me.
Let the kids get up in Switzerland
...or Memphis, Tennessee.

Let the kids get up in Alaska

...and in China.

I don't care.

Let the kids get up in Italy.

Let the kids get up in Spain.

Let them get up in Massachusetts

and Connecticut and Maine.

Let the kids get up in London

and in Paris and Berlin.

Let them get up all they want to.

But not me.

I'm sleeping in.

I've never been so sleepy
since I can't remember when.

You can take away my breakfast.
Give my egg back to the hen.

Nobody's going to get me up,
no matter what he does.

Today's my day for
WOOZY–SNOOZY
ZIZZ–ZIZZ
ZIZZ
ZAZZ
ZUZZ.

You can tickle my feet.
You can shake my bed.

You can pour cold water on my head.

But you're wasting your time.

So go away!

I am NOT going to get up today!

In bed is where I'm going to stay.

And I don't care what the neighbours say!

I never liked them anyway.

Let them try to wake me.

Let them scream and yowl and yelp.

They can yelp from now till Christmas

but it isn't going to help.

My bed is warm.

My pillow's deep.

Today's the day I'm going to sleep.

I don't choose to be up walking.
I don't choose to be up talking.
The only thing I'm choosing
is to lie here woozy-snoozing.

So won't you kindly go away.
I am NOT going to get up today!

You won't get me up
with a Strawberry Flip.
You won't get me up
with a Marshmallow Dip
or a Pineapple Butterscotch Ding Dang Doo!
My tongue is asleep.
And my teeth are too.

You can try with dogs and roosters.
You can try with goats and geese.
But I'm going to go on snoozing.
You can bring in the police.

You can print it in the papers.

Spread the news all over town.

But nothing's going to get me up.

Today I'm staying down.

You can shoot at me with peas and beans!
You can bring in the United States Marines!

You can put the whole thing on TV.
But I won't get up today!
Not me!

Nothing's going to get me up.
Why can't you understand!
You'll only waste your money
if you hire a big brass band.

That's why I say,

"Please go away!

I am NOT going to get up today!"

I guess he really means it.

So you can have the egg.